To

·····························

HAPPY EASTER

Love from,

·····························

The Easter Egg Hunt in MY TOWN

Written by Laura Baker   Illustrated by Jo Parry

HOMETOWN
WORLD

Hop, hop, hooray—it's Easter time!
Bunny bounces out of bed,
feeling grateful for this day,
and everything ahead.

Home Sweet Home

Mommy Bunny smiles and says:
"Springtime's in the air.
Time to search for eggs and love.
We'll find them everywhere!"

Will YOU help them look too?

Just outside a nearby farm,
they search up, down... everywhere!
Hopping along, paw in paw,
Bunny says: "How about over there?"

Playful lambs call over,
with a kind and happy bleat.
"Happy Easter, woolly friends–
Look! Our first Easter treat!"

SPRINGTIME
FARM

With one egg in the basket,
the bunnies stop beside a brook.
Perhaps the egg is in the reeds?
Oh, which way should they look?

Ducklings splash, quack, and wave.
"Maybe try along the water!"
Bunny's thankful for the help:
"Now, I'm a real egg spotter!"

Two eggs in the basket,
the pace is picking up!
And when the bunnies reach a chicken coop,
they're greeted with a "Cluck!"

"We can't stay long," Little Bunny says,
"although visiting is so sweet.
We have lots of eggs to find—
is that one underneath?"

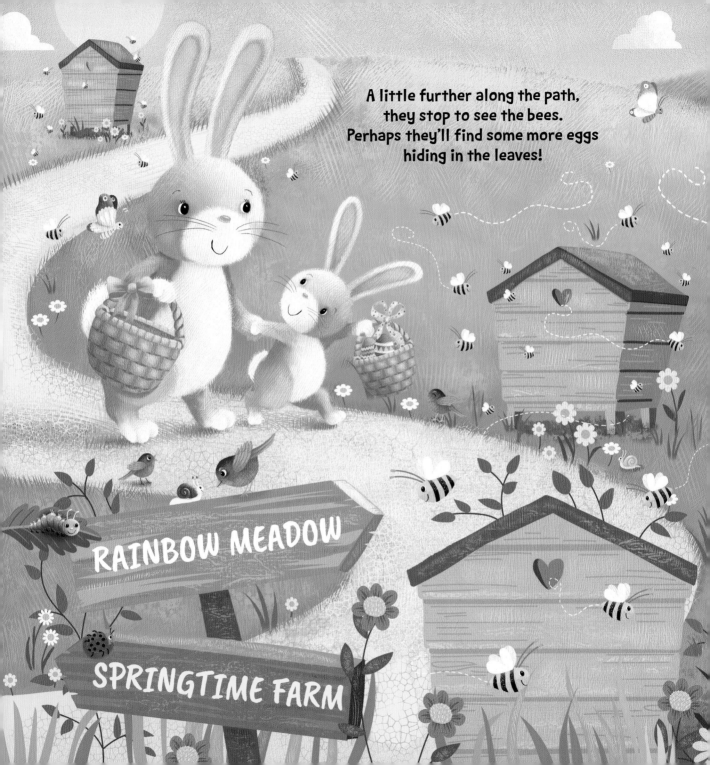

A little further along the path,
they stop to see the bees.
Perhaps they'll find some more eggs
hiding in the leaves!

RAINBOW MEADOW

SPRINGTIME FARM

They stop and smell the flowers
in the field around the hive.
Counting: "One, two, three... there's four!
Now on to find egg five!"

The bunnies take a quiet pause
as a rainbow fills the sky.
Mommy watches fondly
while Bunny looks nearby.

They cuddle and give thanks
for the blessings of the day.
Then clever Bunny spots it—
"A pink one now, hooray!"

At the town's Easter market,
they meet lots of friendly faces.
The bunnies search and peep for eggs
through all their favorite places.

At a park, not far away, there's a spot to take a seat.
Even eggs-pert treasure hunters must stop to rest their feet.

"Have you seen any eggs?" Bunny asks a family.
"Why yes," smiles Raccoon. "Look up there in that tree!"

Happy Easter

HAPPY EASTER!

In puddles with the piggies, Bunny splashes all around.
"Over here," calls Mommy. "Another egg to be found!"

"Let's search for more!" cries Bunny,
and then they dash away...

...to Muddy Paws Farm,
where more friends want to play!

Bright-eyed pups play hide-and-seek
in the farmer's field.
What's that pup sniffing there?
A new egg is revealed!

The sun in the golden sky is setting for the day,
and Little Bunny takes this chance to hop about and play.
With an Easter basket full, and a joyful, grateful heart,
Bunny's ready to be home—right back to the start.

Back through the puppy field-woof, woof, jump.

Back through the puddles-oink, oink, grunt.

Back past the picnic—crunch, crunch, yum.

Back past the market—the busy day is done.

Back past the ponies—neigh, neigh... "Whee!"

Back through the chicken coop—cheep, cheep... "Follow me!"

Back past the brook—quack, quack... "Come!"

Back to the rolling meadow—baa, baa... "Run!"

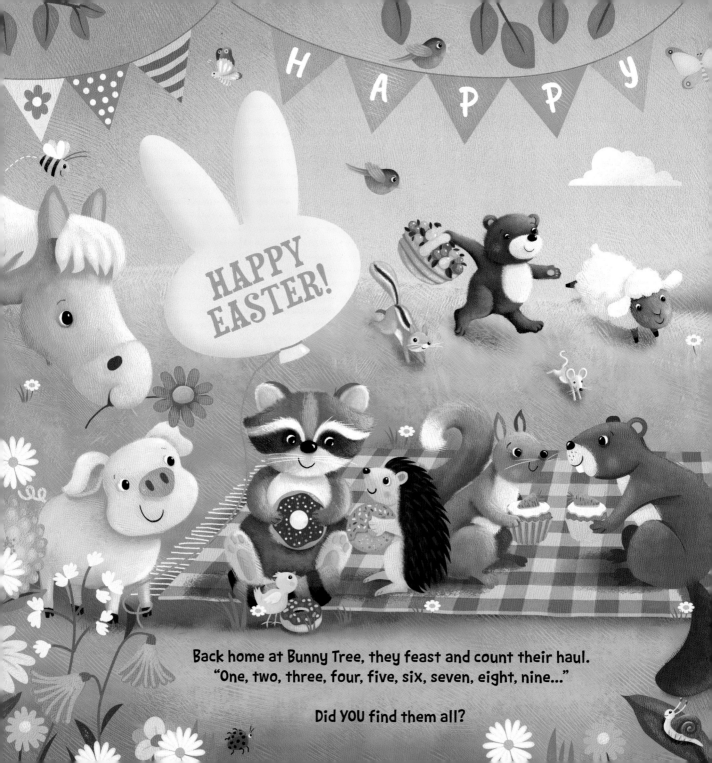

Back home at Bunny Tree, they feast and count their haul.
"One, two, three, four, five, six, seven, eight, nine..."

Did YOU find them all?

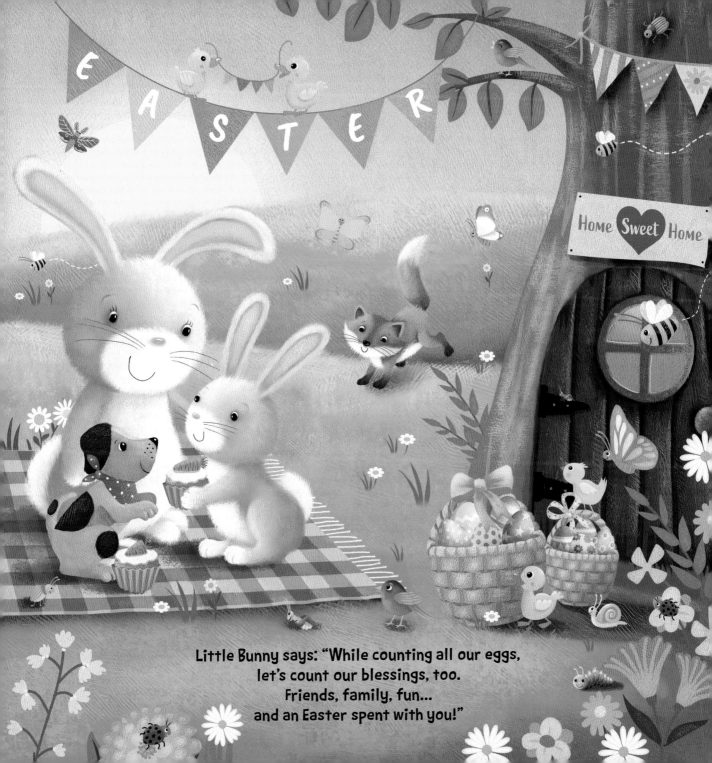

Little Bunny says: "While counting all our eggs,
let's count our blessings, too.
Friends, family, fun...
and an Easter spent with you!"

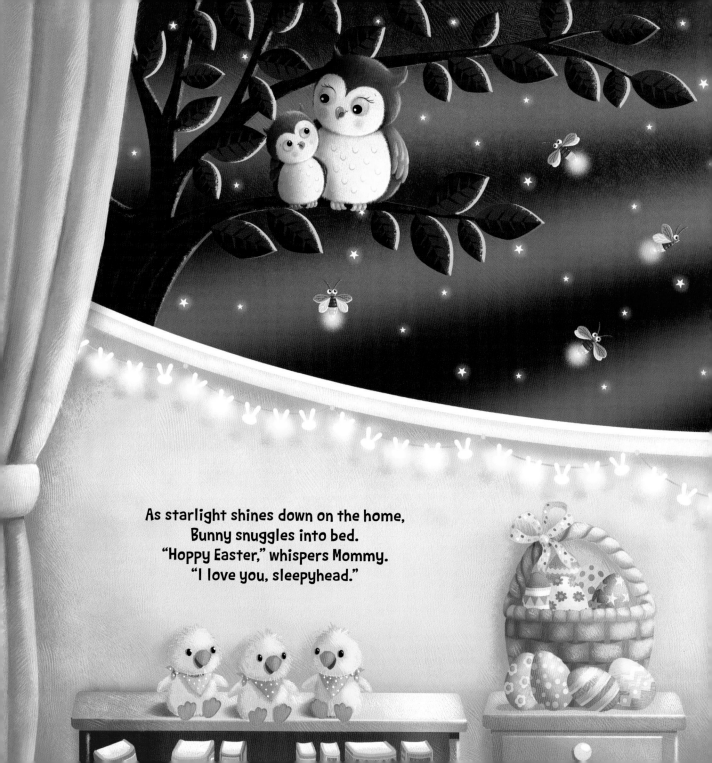

As starlight shines down on the home,
Bunny snuggles into bed.
"Hoppy Easter," whispers Mommy.
"I love you, sleepyhead."

Written by Laura Baker
Illustrated by Jo Parry
Designed by Ryan Dunn

Published by Hometown World,
an imprint of Sourcebooks Kids
P.O. Box 4410, Naperville, Illinois 60567-4410
(630) 961-3900
hometownworld.com
sourcebookskids.com

Source of Production: 1010 Asia Limited,
North Point, Hong Kong, China
Date of Production: July 2022
Run Number: 5026279
Printed and bound in China (OGP)
10 9 8 7 6 5 4 3 2 1

HAPPY EASTER!